The Boxcar Children Mysteries

The Boxcar Children
Surprise Island
The Yellow House
  Mystery
Mystery Ranch
Mike's Mystery
Blue Bay Mystery
The Woodshed Mystery
The Lighthouse
  Mystery
Mountain Top Mystery
Schoolhouse Mystery
Caboose Mystery
Houseboat Mystery
Snowbound Mystery
Tree House Mystery
Bicycle Mystery
Mystery in the Sand
Mystery Behind the
  Wall
Bus Station Mystery
Benny Uncovers a
  Mystery
The Haunted Cabin
  Mystery
The Deserted Library
  Mystery

The Animal Shelter
  Mystery
The Old Motel
  Mystery
The Mystery of the
  Hidden Painting
The Amusement Park
  Mystery
The Mystery of the
  Mixed-Up Zoo
The Camp-out Mystery
The Mystery Girl
The Mystery Cruise
The Disappearing
  Friend Mystery
The Mystery of the
  Singing Ghost
Mystery in the Snow
The Pizza Mystery
The Mystery Horse
The Mystery at the
  Dog Show
The Castle Mystery
The Mystery of the
  Lost Village

THE MYSTERY OF THE LOST VILLAGE

created by
GERTRUDE CHANDLER WARNER

Illustrated by Charles Tang

ALBERT WHITMAN & Company
Morton Grove, Illinois

ISBN 0-8075-5401-4

1 3 5 7 9 10 8 6 4 2

Printed in the U.S.A.

Contents

CHAPTER 1

A New Adventure

"Are you ready for a new adventure?" Grandfather Alden asked with a twinkle in his eyes. It was nearly dusk, and the four Alden children were sitting in the living room playing Go Fish with Mrs. McGregor, the family housekeeper.

"What kind of adventure?" six-year-old Benny asked excitedly. He jumped to his feet, scattering cards everywhere. "Is it a scary adventure or a fun adventure, or is it — ?" He stopped abruptly when his older sister, Violet, tugged on his arm.

1

"Why don't you let Grandfather tell us?" She gently pulled her younger brother back into his seat.

"Well, I'll give you a hint," Grandfather said, settling down on the sofa. "It's not scary, but it's definitely going to be fun. It's something you've never done before. Oh, yes, there's one more thing. You're going to a very exciting place."

"Ever since we moved in with you, Grandfather, we've had one adventure after another!" Henry said. At fourteen, he was the oldest of the four Alden children. He remembered how their lives had changed since the days when they were living in a boxcar. Grandfather Alden had found them and given them a real home with lots of love.

"This may be the most unusual adventure of all," Grandfather said. "You're going to spend two weeks on a Navajo Indian reservation."

"A Navajo reservation!" Ten-year-old Violet cried. "Thank you, Grandfather." A shy, sweet girl, she leaned over and gave her grandfather a big hug.

"How did you arrange it, Grandfather?" Jessie asked. She was two years older than her sister, and very practical. "I thought that only members of a tribe could live on a Native American reservation."

"Don't worry, Jessie," Grandfather reassured her. "You're going to be special guests. My friend, Ed Talbot, invited me to do some trout fishing in the mountains. He told me there's going to be a Pow-Wow at a nearby reservation, and he thought you might like to be part of it."

"You bet we would! A Pow-Wow!" Benny jumped up again, nearly tripping over Watch, the family dog. "I know what a Pow-Wow is. It's like a big fair, only better!"

"I think it means a celebration, sort of a family reunion," Henry said slowly.

"That's right," Grandfather agreed. "Ed told me it's like a gathering of friends and relatives. There will be lots of singing, and dancing, and friends from other tribes are invited. Usually the townspeople come, too. It's a way to learn about the customs and traditions of the Navajo people."

"Where will we stay?" Violet asked.

"Ed has some friends on the reservation, the Lightfeathers. They've invited you to stay in their home with their two children, Joe and Amy. Joe's twelve and Amy's ten."

"It sounds like fun," Violet said. "When do we leave, Grandfather?"

"To get there in time for the Pow-Wow preparations, we have to catch an early morning flight tomorrow," Grandfather said. "Do you think you'll have time to pack tonight?"

"We will if we get started right away," Jessie said. She stood up and began thinking about what they would need. Probably plenty of shorts and tops, she decided, and some jeans and sweaters in case the nights were chilly.

"Okay," Benny said eagerly. He raced upstairs to his room and tossed his duffel bag on the bed. He was busily sorting through his T-shirts when Mrs. McGregor stuck her head around the doorway.

"Be sure to take your hiking boots, Benny. Your grandfather said you'll be doing some hiking on mountain trails."

"I'll pack them right now!" He threw open his closet door and rummaged through a pile of sneakers until he found his hiking boots. Watch strolled in, tail wagging, and plunked himself down on Benny's bed.

"I can't play with you now, Watch," Benny said. "There's just too much to do." Mountain trails, horses, and a Navajo reservation! Benny took a deep breath and stuffed his bathing suit into the bottom of the duffel bag. Half an hour later, he was all packed and happily stretched out next to Watch, patting the dog's stomach. He wished they could leave for the reservation that very minute. Morning seemed such a long way off!

The air was nippy the next day when they set off for the airport. Mrs. McGregor was driving Grandfather's station wagon, and Violet was wedged in the back seat between Henry, Benny, and Watch.

"Are you sure we can't bring Watch on the plane?" Benny asked when they pulled up in front of the terminal.

"No, I think Watch will be happy with Mrs. McGregor," Grandfather said. "She'll make sure he gets plenty of exercise."

"And plenty of play time," Benny said. "He likes to run around outside."

"Don't worry, Benny. I'll take good care of him. Have fun, everyone!" Mrs. Mc-Gregor called as they unloaded the luggage from the car.

A few minutes later, the Aldens checked their baggage at the airline counter and waited for their flight to be announced. Benny spent the next half hour watching sleek, silver planes take off, until Grandfather finally stood up. "That's our flight," he said. The children trooped after him as he handed the tickets to a flight attendant and boarded the plane.

"This is fun!" Benny said, settling into his seat. He kept his nose pressed against the window as the plane taxied down the runway and then took off. It was a clear day and, after lunch, Jessie leaned over and pointed out the Mississippi River to him. Later, he nudged her excitedly. "I think that's the

Grand Canyon!" he said.

"Pretty soon we'll be in New Mexico, and you'll see real cactus plants," Henry said.

Once the plane landed, Grandfather ushered everyone into a taxi. The sun was setting in a blaze of color when they drove down a twisting road and saw a group of beige stucco ranch houses nestled at the foot of a mountain range. A split-rail fence ran around a part of the reservation, and two children rushed to open the gate when they approached. The girl gave a shy smile when Grandfather asked them if they knew the way to the Lightfeathers'.

"We sure do," the boy piped up. "I'm Joe Lightfeather and this is my sister, Amy. We've been waiting for you."

"Do you want to get in and show us the way?" Violet asked. "We can all fit in, if we put down the extra seat."

"Okay," Joe replied as he and Amy scrambled into the taxi.

"Oh, it's beautiful," Jessie said when they pulled up in front of a cozy adobe house with a red tile roof. There were clay pots full of

cactus plants on the front steps, and a giant ficus tree shaded the front lawn. A man and woman hurried out to greet them.

"You must be the Aldens," the woman said. She shook hands with Grandfather and the children as they stepped out of the taxi. "I'm Toni Lightfeather, and this is my husband, Bob. Welcome to our home."

"We have a cat named Snowball. I hope you like animals," Amy said softly to Violet.

Grandfather asked the taxi driver to wait while he chatted with the Lightfeathers for a few minutes. Then he looked at the darkening sky. "I think I'd better be on my way now. Ed's cabin is about an hour's drive from here."

"Aren't you staying for dinner?" Joe asked, surprised. "You should see what Mom's fixing. She made all my favorite foods — fried chicken and stuffing, mashed potatoes, and chocolate layer cake."

"Those are my favorites, too!" Benny exclaimed, and everyone laughed.

"I appreciate the invitation," Grandfather said, "but Ed's expecting me for dinner." He hugged each of the Aldens. "Have a wonderful time, children."

"You, too, Grandfather," Violet said. She felt a little sad that Grandfather was leaving, but she knew she'd enjoy herself at the Lightfeathers'. Amy and Joe looked very friendly, and she could hardly wait to ask if they had any horses. They waved until Grandfather's taxi was out of sight, and then turned toward the house.

"Oh, here he is," Amy said, scooping up a large white cat who had scampered out from under a bush. "Violet, meet Snowball. You can hold him, if you'd like. He likes to be scratched under his chin."

Violet cradled the cat in her arms and he began to purr loudly. "That means he's happy," Amy said.

"Maybe it means he's hungry," Benny said hopefully.

Mrs. Lightfeather laughed. "I have the feeling that you're the one who's hungry, young man. Would you like to help me in the kitchen while everyone else puts the suitcases away?"

"Sure," Benny said eagerly.

"You and Henry will be sleeping in Joe's room, and the girls can stay with Amy," Mr. Lightfeather said.

While the rest of the Aldens trooped into the house and made their way upstairs, Benny followed Mrs. Lightfeather into the kitchen. It was light and airy and filled with hanging baskets of green herbs.

"I'm going to let you make a big decision, Benny," Mrs. Lightfeather said. "Joe told you I made a chocolate layer cake today, but my husband made peach ice cream for dessert. He wanted to surprise me. What shall we do?"

"That's easy," Benny said quickly. "We can have both!"

"Two desserts?" Mrs. Lightfeather said doubtfully.

Benny rubbed his stomach. "If there are any leftovers, I promise to eat them."

Mrs. Lightfeather grinned. "You've got a deal."

CHAPTER 2

Meeting Kinowok

"I love your room," Jessie exclaimed a few minutes later. She and Violet had finished unpacking their suitcases and were admiring the colorful blankets on their twin beds.

"My grandmother made those," Amy said proudly. She was a tall girl with dancing brown eyes and long black hair. "All the colors and designs have a special meaning."

"Look, mine has an eagle on it." Violet peered at a beautiful black-and-white eagle with his wings spread against a pale blue sky.

Amy nodded. "The eagle is a symbol of honor. See that wavy line at the bottom? It stands for the mountains."

"Tell me about mine," Jessie said. "I see a deer and a turtle and some kind of a bird."

"That's a hawk," Amy explained. "He stands for swiftness. The deer means love, and the turtle is used in a lot of Indian designs. He's supposed to be wise."

"Wise?" Jessie said, surprised. "I never think of turtles as being very smart."

Amy smiled. "They live a long time, don't they?"

"I'd love to make one of these," Violet said eagerly. "Are they hard to do?"

"Very hard. In the old days, Navajo women had to shear their own sheep to get the wool. Then they made dyes from berries to color it."

"It's perfect," Jessie said admiringly.

"No, that's the funny part," Amy piped up. "There's always a tiny mistake in the design. The Navajo women put it in on purpose. They thought if it was too perfect, it would offend the gods."

"Really? I don't see any mistake in mine," Violet said.

Amy laughed. "I never could find it, either." She headed for the door. "I think we'd better go down to dinner now."

"Good, I'm starving!" Jessie said.

"We invited a special guest to welcome all the Aldens to the reservation," Mr. Lightfeather said a few minutes later. He was standing at the head of the dining-room table, next to a small wiry man with leathery skin as brown as a chestnut. "This is Kinowok, the oldest man on the reservation, and our storyteller."

"A storyteller!" Benny said excitedly. "I bet you know a zillion stories."

Kinowok smiled as Mr. Lightfeather helped him into his chair. "I've never counted them," he said in a surprisingly strong voice. "But if you stay long enough, you shall hear many."

"What kind of stories do you tell?" Henry asked, as everyone sat down. "Do you know any mysteries?"

Kinowok spread his palms in a graceful

gesture. "Everything around us is a mystery. It all depends on how you look at it."

"That sounds like a riddle," Benny said, as Amy passed him a giant bowl of mashed potatoes.

"Let me explain," Kinowok said, settling back in his chair. "I live at the edge of the reservation, in the foothills. When I walked here tonight, I stumbled across a mystery. I saw some blades of grass that were crushed and some broken dry sticks." He paused. "What did it mean? Can you solve the mystery, young man?" he asked Henry.

Henry hesitated. How could some dry sticks and blades of grass be a mystery? "I guess not, sir," he said finally.

Kinowok gave a broad smile and turned to Joe, who was sitting next to his sister, Amy. "Joe, can you explain it?"

"It might have been a deer running through the brush," Joe said. "He could have crushed the grass and broken the sticks. You'd know for sure if you spotted his tracks."

"Wow, I never thought of that," Benny said, impressed.

"Can you tell your friends anything else?" Kinowok continued. "Let's suppose that I did see tracks."

Joe thought. "Well, you could look at the footprints and tell right away if the deer is male or female. The female has sharper hooves and narrower feet, and the male has a rounded point on his hooves."

Benny was so surprised he nearly forgot to eat. Imagine telling all that just from a footprint!

"And you can tell a lot just from his toe prints," Amy said.

"Toe prints?" Violet asked. "I never heard of such a thing."

"It's true," Amy insisted. "If the toes are spread apart, it means the deer was just running around playing. But if the toes are tight together, it means it was running for its life."

"There are many other mysteries nearby," Kinowok said. "But you have to know where to look."

"What other mysteries?" Benny leaned forward. He didn't want to miss a single word.

"When I was a boy," Kinowok said, "my grandfather told me about a tribal village nearby. It existed a long, long time ago, and its people were peaceful and prosperous. But one summer there was a drought, and the river dried up."

"Then what happened?" Violet asked.

Kinowok shrugged. "Without water, the people could not survive, so the families left. Soon the whole village was overrun with grass and weeds, and now it's buried. Just as though the earth had swallowed it up."

"A lost village," Henry said suddenly. "I just finished reading a book about archaeology, which is the study of ancient peoples. It said that sometimes you can find clues if you know where to start digging."

"Could we look for the village?" Jessie asked. "How close is it?"

"Closer than you think," Kinowok answered. "According to my grandfather, it's just a few feet away."

"It's part of the reservation?" Mr. Light-feather asked.

"No, but it borders on our land. It's hidden somewhere deep in the forest, next to us," Kinowok said. "Some people doubt that the village ever existed. But I have never doubted."

"Wow," said Benny. "I bet we could find it and dig it up if we really tried."

"Archaeology is harder than you think, Benny," Henry said. "You can't just dig things up without knowing what you're doing."

"But we could learn, couldn't we?" Amy pleaded. "Mom, you studied archaeology in college, didn't you?"

"That was a long time ago," Mrs. Light-feather said. "But I spent a couple of summers working on digs, and I can give you some hints, if you like. As a matter of fact, once in a while some students have tried to find the lost village. They never did find it, however. Henry is right, though, it *is* hard." She smiled. "Why don't we talk about it tomorrow morning?"

"Then we can start digging!" Joe said.

"Sounds great!" said Jessie.

"A Pow-Wow *and* a lost village," Benny said. "This could be our best adventure ever!"

"A village never disappears completely," Mrs. Lightfeather said the next morning. The Aldens were sitting around the oak breakfast table with Joe and Amy, drinking orange juice. "There are always traces left behind, and the trick is to find them. That's what archaeology is all about."

"What sort of traces?" Benny asked.

"It could be a cooking pot, or maybe an arrowhead, or a handful of colored beads. The important thing is to be very careful and not destroy something important." She opened a cardboard box and pointed to some small digging tools and brushes. "You can dig with these trowels, and then use the sifter to catch any fragments you find in the soil."

"Why do you have a paintbrush in there?" Benny asked.

"That's not a paintbrush," Henry said. "You use that to brush dirt off the objects carefully, instead of just yanking them out of the ground. That way you don't damage them."

"That's right," Mrs. Lightfeather said. "Take the tools with you this morning, and remember that an archaeologist is like a detective. You have to look for clues, and put the pieces together. And here's a box to hold any treasures you may find."

Half an hour later, the four Aldens, along with Joe and Amy, were making their way deep into the forest.

"I wonder how much of the village is left," Violet said.

"Probably not much," Jessie spoke up. "Where should we start digging?"

"I've found a lot of arrowheads straight ahead in that clearing," Joe said. "But that doesn't mean there's a village."

"Then let's start there," Jessie said eagerly. "Though I'm not sure I'd even recognize an arrowhead if I saw one."

"Kinowok taught me a lot about them." When they reached the clearing, Joe hunched down in the soft earth and opened the box of tools. "He can even tell what tribe they're from."

"We should start by making a grid," Henry said. "That's the way real archaeologists work."

"A grid?" Benny was puzzled.

Henry drew several lines in the dirt with the end of a stick. "You see, if we divide the area up into squares, we can make sure we don't go over the same place twice."

"That's a good idea," Violet said. "I'll take this square."

For the next two hours, the children worked steadily, scraping away layers of dirt with the trowels.

"Look, Jessie," Amy said, nudging her. "I think you've found an arrowhead. Or at least part of one."

"Are you sure?" Jessie picked up a piece of gray stone and dusted it off.

"That's an arrowhead, all right," Joe said happily.

"It just looks like a plain old stone," Jessie looked disappointed.

"Someone spent a long time making it,"

Joe told her. He turned it over in his palm. "See all those little chips along the sides? You make those with a pointed hammer. Every time you hit the edge, a tiny flake flies off. And you have to make sure each little chip touches the next."

Jessie ran her finger carefully along the edge, and drew back. "It's really sharp."

"Look," Benny said excitedly, a little while later. "I found something!" He plucked a piece of bright orange pottery out of the dirt. "I think it's part of a plate, or maybe a bowl."

"It has a Navajo design on it," Amy said. "See those two tents put together to form a diamond? That stands for north, south, east and west. The four points of the compass."

"I bet we're standing right over the lost village!" Benny said, reaching for the trowel. "I want to keep working all day."

Amy laughed. "Don't you want to take a break for lunch? We packed chicken sand-wiches, and I have a thermos of lemonade."

Benny looked up with interest. "Maybe a quick break," he said eagerly.

* * *

It was late afternoon when the children returned to the Lightfeather home. Amy raced into the kitchen to show her mother their treasures.

"Jessie found an arrowhead, and Benny found some pottery," she exclaimed. "I think we're really on the trail of the ancient village, Mom."

Mrs. Lightfeather gave a sad smile. "I'm happy that you enjoyed your dig, but I'm afraid your days there are numbered."

"What do you mean?" Amy asked.

"We had a council meeting this morning, and it seems that a real estate developer is trying to take over the forest. He wants to build vacation homes there."

"He's going to chop down all those trees?" Joe asked.

"That's right, if he gets a permit from the local government." Mrs. Lightfeather poured tall glasses of juice for everyone. "So enjoy the forest while you can. There will be bulldozers there in a couple of weeks."

"Isn't there anything we can do to stop them?" Henry asked.

Mrs. Lightfeather looked thoughtful. "Well, if there's really a village buried on that land, the real estate developer would have to stop, and archaeologists would excavate the site. That's the law. But first you'd have to prove it's really a historic site."

"Then we'll have to work harder than ever," Amy promised. She looked at her new friends, the Aldens. "Let's go to the dig every single day," she said.

"Count us in," Henry told her. "If there really is a lost village, we've got two weeks to find it."

CHAPTER 3

Working at the Dig

"Is everybody ready for another day at the dig?" Amy asked at breakfast the next morning.

"We're all set," Henry said, finishing a big plate of bacon and eggs.

"Benny helped me pack sandwiches and a thermos of cider," Joe added, pointing to a picnic basket. "We can work until sundown, if we want to."

The six children were just heading out the front door when they nearly collided with a young man dressed in jeans and denim.

"Is Mrs. Lightfeather at home?" he asked politely. "I'm Michael Running Deer."

"You must be new on the reservation," Amy said, staring at the stranger.

"He's not from the reservation," Mrs. Lightfeather said, suddenly appearing in the front hall. "You didn't waste any time," she said, handing him a batch of official-looking papers. "This will show you the exact boundaries of the reservation."

"Thanks," the young man said, tucking the papers under his arm. "The bulldozers will be here before we know it," he added heading down the front walk.

"Mom, who was that?" Joe asked, concerned.

His mother sighed. "Michael Running Deer works for the real estate developer," she said sadly. "I'm afraid we're very close to losing the forest."

"Then let's get going," Benny said, barreling out the door. "Maybe we can find the lost village today!"

Mrs. Lightfeather smiled. "That would be wonderful, Benny, but don't count on it."

It was a bright, sunny day and, by mid-morning, Henry and Joe decided to take a break. They had just settled down on a log to drink some cider, when they were surprised by a young woman in a nice dress and high heels, with a video camera slung over her shoulder.

"Oh," she said, startled. "I didn't expect to find anybody here." She looked at the grid Henry had drawn in the soft earth, and the mounds of dirt that the children had overturned. "I guess I should introduce myself," she said in a friendly voice. "I'm Rita Neville."

"I'm Henry Alden and this is my friend, Joe Lightfeather," Henry told her.

"What are they doing?" the woman asked, pointing to Jessie and Amy who were vigorously digging with their trowels.

Henry hesitated. The lost village was a secret, and he knew that Joe didn't feel like sharing it with anyone.

"It looks like a treasure hunt," she prompted, when no one answered her.

"It's more like a scavenger hunt," Joe said

finally. "We're playing a game."

"Well, have fun." She took another quick look at the dig and turned to leave. "I've got to get back to work now." Her high heels sank into the soft earth, and she nearly stumbled.

"Excuse me, but what are you working on?" Joe asked.

"I'm a television producer," she said brightly. She patted her camera case. "I'm planning a documentary on Indian life, and I need some location shots."

"But this isn't part of the reservation," Henry told her.

"Oh, I know," she said quickly. "I just felt like taking a hike. I'm staying at Morton's Motel."

"What did you think of her?" Henry asked when Rita Neville was out of earshot.

Joe shrugged. "I don't think she wandered here by mistake. Nobody goes for a hike dressed up like that."

"You're right. There isn't even a path." He squinted at the midday sun, just as Violet called to him from the dig.

"Hey, break time is over!" she teased him.

Henry nodded. "I guess we should get back to work."

It was late afternoon when Violet squealed in surprise. "Look what I found!" she said, pointing to a dark red circle in the dirt.

"What is it?" Jessie asked.

"I think it's the rim of a plate, or bowl," Henry said excitedly. "And it looks like it's not even broken. You'll have to be careful getting it out in one piece."

"I'm going to take my time," Violet said. She hunched over her find and began brushing away layers of earth. After a few minutes, she sank back on her heels. "There it is!"

"It's beautiful," Jessie told her. Together they lifted the large earthenware bowl out of the sandy soil. "And there's not even a single chip on it."

"Violet, I think you found something important," Joe said.

"I want to find a bowl, too!" Benny said eagerly.

Amy laughed. "All right, Benny. But I don't think we'll be lucky twice in one day."

* * *

At the end of the day's work, the four Aldens were tired, but happy. After congratulating Violet on finding the bowl, Mrs. Lightfeather talked about plans for the Pow-Wow.

"We really need to get started on a project. The Pow-Wow is only a week away," she said. She turned to the Aldens. "Who wants to be my helper?"

"I'll volunteer!" Violet spoke up. "What are we going to make?"

"Corn pudding."

"Corn pudding?" Benny wrinkled his nose.

"You'll love it," Amy promised. "It's got cornmeal, molasses, and lots of spices. Mom makes it on the stove, but in the old days, it would have cooked for hours over the fire."

"What about us? What can we do?" Benny spoke up.

"You and Henry can help me make some belts," Joe said. "I've already cut the leather and made the buckles, but there's lots of bead work to do."

"You're making belts?" Benny looked surprised. "Why not just buy some?"

Joe laughed. "You can't buy belts like these. Each one is handmade, and they all have designs from our tribe." He turned to Henry. "We can get started after dinner tonight."

Later that evening, Amy took Violet and Jessie to see her Appaloosa pony named Thunder. It was a short walk from the Lightfeathers' house to the reservation's stable, and Thunder whinnied with pleasure when he saw the girls.

"He's really gentle," Amy said. She held up a plastic bag filled with apple slices. "This is his favorite treat. You can feed him, if you want to."

"Could we ride him sometime?" Jessie asked.

"Maybe tomorrow," Amy said. "After we work at the dig. I'm really getting excited about it, aren't you?"

Violet was about to answer when a noise behind her made her jump.

"Sorry, girls," said a tall blond man in his

early thirties. "I didn't mean to startle you."
He had come into the stable so quietly that
they hadn't heard him. "Nice horse," he
added, patting Thunder on the neck. "Pinto,
right?"

"He's an Appaloosa," Amy corrected him.
She stared at him, puzzled. She knew he
didn't live on the reservation.

"You're probably wondering what I'm
doing here," he said casually. "I'm Ted
Clark. I'm a genealogist." He grinned at the
blank looks on the girls' faces. "A genealogist
is someone who traces family trees."

"Do you mean grandparents and great-
grandparents?" Amy asked.

"Even further back than that. I'm hoping
to go back five or six generations in my family. The council gave me permission to look
through their records."

"Oh," Amy said, understanding. "You're
a Navajo?"

"Partly," Ted Clark said. "Most of my
family, I mean my ancestors, come from the
northeast. Places like Maine and New
Hampshire."

"Welcome to the reservation," Amy said.

"Thanks. Nice necklace you're wearing," he said, noticing the heavy silver strand around Amy's neck. "That's a pretty stone in the center. An opal, right?"

Amy touched the bright blue stone. "No, it's a turquoise."

"Oh, I've never seen one before. Well, I'd better get going. I'm staying at the motel in town, and I've got a lot of work to do. Nice to meet you."

After he left, Jessie and Violet fed Thunder while Amy used a curry brush to smooth his mane.

"Something's wrong," Amy said quietly.

"What?" Jessie looked up as Thunder nuzzled her hand.

"Ted Clark." She shook her head. "He said he's part Navajo, but he couldn't even recognize a piece of turquoise."

Jessie shrugged. "Maybe he doesn't know much about stones."

"It's more than that," Amy persisted. She touched the blue stone around her neck. "Turquoise is very important to my people, and we use it in a lot of our jewelry. There's even a legend about it."

"Oh, tell us," Violet said. She loved stories and enjoyed hearing tales about the Navajo people.

"I guess you'd call it a fairy tale. Once there was a woman who found a beautiful blue stone — a piece of turquoise. It was the prettiest stone she had ever seen, and she took it to the top of a high mountain. When she set it down, it turned into a goddess right before her eyes." She paused. "I've heard that story ever since I was a little girl. I wonder why Ted Clark had never heard it."

After they locked the stable, the three girls headed back to the Lightfeather house.

"Jessie, I just realized something," Amy said. "You don't have a project for the Pow-Wow. Would you like to do an Indian dance with me?"

"An Indian dance?" Jessie repeated. "Would I be allowed to?"

"We can talk to Kinowok, but I'm sure he'll say yes. At the Pow-Wow, we can explain that you're not a Navajo, but you're a guest. When we dance at the Pow-Wow, sometimes guests join in. It's our way of sharing our customs with the townspeople."

"It sounds like fun, but . . ." Jessie hesitated. "Do you think I'll be able to learn the dance in time to perform it?"

Amy nodded. "The dance is very simple. The hard part is making the regalia."

"What's regalia?" Violet asked.

"It's an authentic Navajo dress from the old days. You would probably call it a costume, but we call it regalia. Don't worry, Jessie," she said encouragingly. "I'll help you with it."

Later that evening, Jessie noticed Henry and Joe sifting through boxes of colored beads on the dining-room table. Benny was frowning over a pad of graph paper, nibbling the end of his pencil.

"What are you doing?" Jessie asked curiously.

"We're working on our beaded belts, but I can't think of what to draw. Joe says that first you make a picture on this special paper, and then you choose the beads. That's the fun part." He pointed to some crumbled-up graph paper. "But I'm stuck. I can't think of anything I want to draw."

Jessie thought for a moment. "What about an eagle?" she asked, thinking of the beautiful design on her bedspread.

Benny brightened. "That's a great idea!" He immediately bent down and began drawing the outline of an eagle with outspread wings.

CHAPTER 4

Footprints

It was two days later when Henry realized that something strange was going on at the dig. "I just don't get it." He nudged the soft earth with the toe of his shoe. "I worked all yesterday afternoon on this square, and now it's filled in with dirt."

"Maybe you were working on the square next to it," Jessie offered. "It's easy to get confused."

"No, I know it was this one," Henry insisted. "I had gotten through all the topsoil, and I was just starting to find some bits of pottery. Now I've got to start all over!"

Joe squatted back on his heels. "Somebody filled in my square, too," he said quietly. "And take a look at these tracks." He pointed to a trail of tiny round holes that led around the edge of his dig.

"What kind of tracks? Deer tracks?" Benny jumped up. He thought it would be a lot of fun to be able to identify animal tracks, like Joe and Amy could.

Joe laughed. "I'm afraid not, Benny. These are human tracks."

"They don't look like footprints," Violet said. "Some of them are too little and round."

"That's because they're made from a woman's high-heeled shoes," Amy explained.

"Ms. Neville!" Henry exclaimed. "Remember the day she came to the dig in those high heels and nearly tripped?"

Joe nodded. "She must have come back to take another look around."

"But why would she want to wander around the dig at night? And why would she fill in the holes we made?" Jessie wondered.

Henry shook his head. "I have no idea. But I think we'd better get back to work."

They were busy with their trowels when something shiny in the dirt caught Benny's eye. Maybe it was a glass bead or part of a hunting knife! "Oh shucks," he said, when he bent down for a closer look. "It's just an old key ring. And there aren't even any keys on it."

"Let's have a look." Henry examined the small red square dangling from a tarnished chain. The letter M was emblazoned on it. "Here, Benny," he said, returning it. "Keep it safe. Maybe we'll find the owner."

"And maybe we'll find out who's been sneaking around the dig," Jessie added.

The sun was setting when the children left the dig and made their way through the forest. A sudden cracking sound from the forest made them jump, and Violet spun around in surprise.

"Sorry to frighten you," Ted Clark said, emerging from behind a tree. He rubbed his ankle and winced. "I'm afraid I tripped over a fallen branch."

"What were you doing in the middle of the forest?" Benny asked curiously.

"Just taking a look around." He paused, glancing at Henry's knapsack. "Are you kids on a hike or something?"

"No, we've just been — " Violet stopped suddenly. Something in Jessie's expression made her cautious. "Playing," she added firmly.

"There's not much place to play around here," Ted said, glancing at the dense forest. He gestured in the direction of the dig. "What's over that way? Anything worth looking at?"

"Just a lot of poison ivy," Joe spoke up. "But if you head over that way" — he pointed away from the dig — "there are some pretty nice trails."

After Ted left, Benny edged closer to Violet. "At least we know that's not *his* key ring. I wish we could find out who 'M' is!"

Violet took his hand. "Me, too."

After dinner that night, Amy and Jessie went upstairs to begin working on their outfits for the Pow-Wow dance.

"We need to make a buckskin dress for you," Amy said. "My mom said you could use this." She opened a cardboard box and laid two sheets of tan buckskin across her bed.

"It's beautiful material," Jessie said. "But how can we make a dress out of it?"

Amy pulled a simple Navajo dress out of her closet. "It's really easy to do. You use one sheet for the front, and one for the back, and then you attach them at the shoulders."

"What do we do about the sides?" Jessie asked.

"That part's easy. We just lace up the sides." She smiled at Jessie's puzzled look. "Don't worry. If we're the same size, we can use my dress as a pattern."

Amy held her dress up to Jessie and nodded. "Just what I thought. This will fit you perfectly." She handed Jessie a pair of scissors and both girls sat on the bed. Amy laid her dress over the buckskin and trimmed the material to match it. "Now all we have to do is make a lot of little cuts down each side."

"Fringe!" Jessie said, pleased.

"Exactly," Amy answered.

At last they were finished. Amy stood up. "Time to try it on," she said. A buckskin thong on each shoulder held the dress together. Amy worked quickly, lacing up the sides while Jessie stood still.

"Now all we need is a cape, and that's really easy." She reached into the box and pulled out a piece of rectangular buckskin with a hole in the center. "Just slip this over your head."

"It feels so soft," Jessie said, running her hand over the smooth skin.

"You'll need these, too." Amy handed her a pair of leggings and moccasins. "I hope we wear the same shoe size," she said.

"They're just right," Jessie said, slipping her feet into the soft red moccasins. "They feel like slippers."

Amy smiled. "Take a look in the mirror, Jessie. With some jewelry and a pouch, you'll look just like a Navajo girl."

"I love it!" Jessie said.

"A Navajo girl would probably sew a lot

of pretty beads on her regalia, but we don't have time for that, since we have to practice the dance. We'll just add a necklace and a few bracelets and you'll be all set."

Meanwhile, Henry and Benny were downstairs admiring Joe's hand-cut leather belts.

"Wow, these are neat," Benny said. He picked up a slender belt of fine tanned leather. "Do you think my eagle will fit on this one, Joe?"

Joe eyed the eagle that Benny had drawn on his graph paper. "I think you need a wider one," he said. "If you know what colors you want to use, you can start doing the bead-work right now."

"How do we get started?" Benny ran his fingers through the dishes of colored beads on the dining-room table.

Joe handed Benny two small blocks of wood and a flat board. "First we have to make the loom, Benny. We're going to nail a block on each end of the board, and then hammer in a row of eight nails across the top and bottom."

"This part is fun," Benny said, as he and Joe worked. When they had finished, Benny looked up expectantly. "Now what?"

"Now cut eight pieces of string. Make sure they're long enough so that you can string them from the top to the bottom of the loom. Once they're fastened good and tight, you can thread a needle and start making rows of beads."

"Okay!" Benny said happily.

"I'll help you thread the needle," Henry said to Benny.

"And I'll help you string the loom," Joe said.

When they had finished, Joe said, "Nice work," examining the homemade loom.

"Thanks. What do I do next?" Benny asked.

"This is the part I like most of all." Joe pointed to the bowls of beads in the center of the table. "Look at your design, and see what color beads you need for each row."

Benny squinted at the graph paper and then burst into a smile. "It's easy," he said proudly. "All I have to do is count the little squares. I need three blue beads, four black beads, and three more blue ones. That will be for the sky and the top of the eagle's head."

"Very good," Joe said. "Just make sure you thread the beads in exactly that order."

Downstairs, Violet was measuring molasses for the Indian pudding. The kitchen was already filled with the rich smells of cinnamon and vanilla.

"This is a very old recipe," Mrs. Lightfeather told her. "My great-grandmother gave it to me." She laughed. "Of course, in the old days, the women would grind their own cornmeal." She reached for a box of cornmeal in the pantry. "Now we can do it the easy way."

"How did your great-grandmother cook?" Violet asked. "She didn't have a stove, did she?"

"No, but she had a campfire. And lots of stoneware pots."

"Like the one I found at the dig!" Violet said.

"Yes, exactly."

Violet was puzzled. "But you said the pot I found was made out of clay. Wouldn't it break if you put it over the fire?"

"Yes, it would," Mrs. Lightfeather said. "So the Navajos had to think of another way of heating their food. And do you know what they did?" When Violet shook her head, she went on: "They heated a stone over the fire and filled the clay pot with water. Then they dropped the stone into the water."

"So the stone made the water hot," Violet said quickly, "and they could cook some of their food that way."

"Exactly." Mrs. Lightfeather sat down at the kitchen table while Violet mixed ingredients in a sky-blue bowl. "You know, Violet," she said, "now that there are two of us doing the cooking, I could probably try a few more recipes to exhibit at the Pow-Wow. Would you like that?"

"I'd like that a lot," Violet told her. She was really enjoying herself at the Lightfeathers.' Joe and Amy were so friendly, and she liked learning new things. "I just realized that there's a design on the bottom of the bowl," she said, lifting the wooden spoon out for a moment.

"That's my grandmother's bowl," Mrs. Lightfeather told her. "It has a thunderbird on the bottom."

"I've never heard of that kind of bird," Violet said, surprised.

"It's not a real bird, but it's a very important symbol to our people. The Navajos used to believe that the thunderbird made thunder by flapping his wings. And when he opened and closed his eyes, lightning flashed across the sky."

Violet knew she had seen the symbol somewhere before, and she frowned, trying to remember. Suddenly it came to her. "Mrs. Lightfeather," she said, "I think there was a thunderbird on the rim of the bowl I found at the dig."

"Really?" Mrs. Lightfeather looked up from an old recipe file.

"A tiny one. And it had its wings outstretched just like this one."

"Why don't you get the bowl and we can look at it again?" Mrs. Lightfeather suggested. "I'll finish the mixing."

Violet raced outside to the patio. After everyone had admired the bowl, she had carefully cleaned it and put it in a sturdy cardboard box in the utility shed. Now she opened the door to the shed, flipped on the light switch, and reeled back in shock. The box was gone!

Violet began searching the shelves, her heart pounding. Could someone have moved it? But who — and why? After a few minutes, she realized her search was hopeless. Her treasure was gone.

CHAPTER 5

Snooping at the Dig

"I can't believe it's gone," Violet said softly to Mrs. Lightfeather a few minutes later. "Who would take it?"

"Someone must have stolen it," Joe said. "Maybe they thought it was valuable." All the children had gathered in the kitchen once they heard what had happened.

"But no one else knows about the bowl," Violet pointed out. "No one else even knows about the dig."

"That's not really true," Henry interrupted. "What about Rita Neville? And Ted

52

Clark? We've run into both of them wandering around in the woods.''

"I knew there was something suspicious about Ted Clark!" Amy blurted out. "He says he's part Navajo, Mom, but he didn't know what turquoise looks like. And he said his relatives are from New England!"

Mrs. Lightfeather looked serious. "I met him yesterday, searching through the council records. If he told you he's from New England, he's way off base. All the Navajo tribes are right here in the Southwest," she said.

"Maybe he was watching from the woods when you found the bowl," Jessie suggested. "And maybe he saw you put it in the tool shed."

"Maybe," Violet said reluctantly. She couldn't believe that someone would steal something she'd worked so hard to find. Yet someone had taken it. Why?

The next morning was bright and sunny, and the children arrived at the dig after breakfast.

"Just as I thought!" Jessie said. She pointed to a square on the left side of the dig. "Someone's been here during the night."

"How do you know?" Benny asked.

"Because I laid a little trap for them." Jessie squatted on her heels and peered at the dirt. "I left two twigs here yesterday afternoon. I crossed them so they formed an X. And now look — they've been pushed aside."

"I think someone's been snooping around my square, too," Henry said, frowning. "The hole is much deeper, and you can see red clay. I know I didn't dig down that far yesterday."

"Who do you think is doing it?" Violet asked. She shivered a little even though the day was warm.

"Probably the same person who took your bowl," Amy said quietly. "And that person could be watching us from the woods right this minute."

"Good morning!" A cheerful voice made the children all turn in surprise. It was Michael Running Deer. He was standing in the center of the path, setting up a metal pole.

"What are you doing?" Benny piped up.

"I'm surveying," Michael answered. "We'll be moving those bulldozers in pretty soon, and I need to get some preliminary work done." He unrolled some blueprints from his back pocket and looked over the dig. "There are always a few last-minute measurements to take before we get the heavy equipment in."

"I'm going to miss the woods," Amy said sadly. "I can't believe all these trees will be cut down in a few weeks."

Michael looked solemn. "I guess you kids have really enjoyed playing here." He stared at the huge tree that towered over them. The sky was bright blue, and the forest had never looked more beautiful.

"It's more than playing," Benny told him. "We're finding things."

"What sort of things?" Michael asked.

"Arrowheads, pieces of pottery," Benny said. "And Violet found a bowl."

"It makes you think about the people who lived here a long time ago, doesn't it?" Michael said. He lifted his binoculars and scanned the forest. "I often wonder about them." He put down his binoculars and his expression was very serious. "But you can't stop progress. Pretty soon, this whole forest will be full of roads and homes." He wiped his face with a bandanna. "Well, I'd better get back to work now."

The children returned to the dig, and Violet looked thoughtful. "It seemed as if something was bothering him," she whispered to Amy.

Amy nodded. "It did. I wonder what?" She crouched over her square at the dig and picked up a trowel.

By mid-afternoon, everyone was tired and thirsty. "I'm ready to take a break," Joe said. "Why don't we go into town for a cold drink?"

"Good idea!" Violet said, scrambling to her feet. She had just packed her trowel in her knapsack when Benny let out a whoop.

"I've found something!" Benny was so excited he was digging in the earth with his bare hands. "It's some kind of bone!"

"Really?" Joe dropped down beside him. "Be careful you don't damage it." He helped Benny smooth away the top layers of soil from his find.

"Here it is," Benny said. He held up a large bone with a big knob at one end. "What is it?" he asked. "Do you think it came from a buffalo?"

Amy leaned closer and started to laugh. "I'm afraid not, Benny. That bone belongs to Honey. She's a cocker spaniel who lives next door to us."

"Honey?" Benny's face fell. "You mean this is a dog bone?"

"I'm afraid so," Joe said. "She loves to bury things and then dig them up. If you look at it carefully, you'll see it's not even a real bone, Benny. It's made out of rawhide." Benny started to toss the bone back into the hole, but Joe stopped him. "Put it in your pocket, Benny. We'll give it to Honey when we get back home."

Half an hour later, all six children trooped into Cranston's, the general store.

"This is my favorite place in town," Amy

confided. "They sell everything from saddles to sunflower seeds. And they make fresh lemonade with crushed ice."

The Aldens were settled with tall glasses of lemonade at a small table in the back of the store when they spotted Rita Neville at the counter.

"She must still be looking for locations for that television show," Violet whispered to Amy.

When Jessie got up to get everyone refills a few minutes later, Ms. Neville was sipping a soft drink. She glanced at Jessie's stained overalls and shook her head.

"I bet you've been playing in the forest today," she said in a friendly way. "Looks like you've been rolling in the dirt."

"We haven't been playing, we've been working," Benny said, suddenly popping up behind Jessie. "We're . . . excavating."

"Oh, and what are you *excavating*?" Ms. Neville sounded as though she were joking.

"All sorts of things," Jessie said vaguely.

"Violet found a really pretty dish, except now it's gone!" Benny piped up.

"That's too bad. Maybe you can buy another one," Rita Neville said.

"This was a special dish," Benny insisted. Jessie tried to catch Benny's eye to make him stop talking, but he ignored her.

Ms. Neville pushed away her drink and looked interested. "Have you found anything else? Any wood carvings? Any silver or turquoise?"

"I don't think so," Benny shrugged.

"Our drinks are ready," Jessie said. She nudged her brother, glad that they had an excuse to escape from Ms. Neville.

"Well, have you or haven't you?" Ms. Neville repeated.

"I told you I don't know," Benny said, putting the drinks on a cardboard tray. "Anyway, I wasn't very lucky today. The only thing I found was an old bone."

"A bone!" Ms. Neville slid off the stool and knelt down so she could talk to Benny eye to eye. "Tell me about it. What did it look like?"

"It was big, and it had a knob at one end — "

"Benny," Jessie interrupted. "I can't carry all these drinks by myself."

"Where did you find the bone? The same place you were digging the other day?"

Benny opened his mouth to answer when Jessie said, *"Benny!"*

"Okay, okay," he said, picking up the tray. He couldn't understand why Ms. Neville was so interested in a dumb old dog bone. "That's right. I found it in the forest," he said over his shoulder to Ms. Neville.

She started to follow Jessie and Benny back to their seats, and then changed her mind. Throwing a dollar bill on the counter, she hurried out of the store.

"She sure was interested in that bone," Benny said when they sat down.

"I wish we could find out what happened to my bowl," Violet said. "It was so pretty, with the bird on one side, and the snake on the other."

"By the way," Jessie said. "Why are there so many snakes on Indian pottery?"

Amy looked up from her lemonade.

"That's because snakes, or serpents, have a special meaning for us."

"I understand why you like birds," Violet said. "But why snakes?"

"We respect them both." Amy looked around the table at her friends. "Birds can soar high into the sky, but snakes are powerful, too. They can shed their skin. Now that's a real mystery!"

"I never thought of it that way," Violet told her.

"Can we stop at the stables on the way home?" Jessie asked. "I'd like to see Thunder again."

"Sure," Amy agreed.

When they stepped outside Cranston's, they spotted Ted Clark, chatting with one of the elders of the tribe.

"Hi, kids," he greeted them. To their surprise, he fell into step with them as they headed to the stables. "I've been doing some research," he said, patting a thick manila folder under his arm.

"What have you learned?" Amy asked.

"Well, I've come across something interesting," he told her. "Did you know that some tribes use a stone to mark buried treasure?"

Amy looked doubtful. "You don't have to be a Navajo to use a stone as a marker."

"Oh, but this isn't an ordinary stone." Ted Clark lowered his voice as if he were telling an important secret. "It's a special stone. It's shaped like a triangle and glows in the dark."

"I've never heard of that," Joe spoke up. "And Kinowok talks about Indian customs all the time."

"It's true," Ted Clark insisted. "Maybe not many people know about it, but it's true."

He said good-bye at the end of the street, and the children headed for the stables. As they rounded the corner, Violet caught a glimpse of Rita Neville. She had been walking behind them the whole time! Was she spying on them?

"Amy," Violet asked when they were inside the stable, "do you believe what Ted said about the stone that glows in the dark?"

Amy shrugged. "I never heard of it before, but it could be true, I guess." She greeted

Thunder, who whinnied softly when he saw them.

"If we could find a stone like that at the dig, it would save us a lot of time." Jessie paused. "We could go look for it tonight."

Meanwhile, the boys refilled Thunder's trough with fresh hay. "So what did you think about the glowing-rock story?" Joe asked.

"I think he made it up," Henry said flatly.

"Me, too," Benny chimed in. "Why would a rock glow in the dark?"

Violet and Amy exchanged a look, and then Amy leaned close to whisper in Amy's ear. "If we go, let's go without the boys. Just us girls."

CHAPTER 6

A Close Call

"This is creepy," Violet said. "And I'm freezing."

"I told you to wear a sweater," Jessie muttered. "The nights get chilly here."

It was midnight and the two sisters were headed for the dig with Amy. Amy swung her flashlight in a zigzag motion to light the way, but the girls still stumbled over stones and fallen tree branches.

The forest looked different at night, Violet thought. Everything was hidden in shadows and strange shapes seemed to hide in the darkness.

Suddenly there was a flutter of wings around her head, and a screeching noise pierced the stillness. "Oh no!" Violet cried, and clutched Jessie's arm. "What was that?"

Amy giggled. "Just a hoot owl, silly." She was feeling a little uneasy herself, but didn't want to show it. She picked her way carefully around a tree stump, and then froze. She heard a twig snap and then another. Someone was walking in the forest with them!

"Shhh." She put her finger to her lips and turned off the flashlight.

"What is it?" Violet whispered.

"Someone's nearby."

Jessie gulped. "Where?" She peered around her, but everything was pitch-black.

"Ahead of us on the path, I think." Amy darted into the shadows and pulled her friends after her. "If we walk fast, we can circle around and come up beside them. But we'll have to be very quiet. Can you do that?"

She looked at Violet, whose teeth were chattering.

"I'll try," Violet promised.

The three girls moved swiftly through the forest, with Amy in the lead. Suddenly she came to a dead stop and started to laugh.

"What in the world — " Jessie began. Amy swung the flashlight in a wide arc, catching Henry, Joe, and Benny silhouetted against the trees. Henry blinked in the light, and then shook his head in disbelief.

"What are you doing here?" he asked, rushing over to the girls.

"What are *you* doing here?" Jessie retorted.

"We're trailing Michael Running Deer," Joe said, moving in closer to them.

"Michael Running Deer!" Jessie was surprised. "You mean, he's prowling around the forest, too?"

"That's right, and we want to find out why," Henry said. "Joe noticed him crossing the field toward the dig, and we jumped out of bed to follow him."

Violet looked at Benny. He had thrown a

flannel jacket over his pajamas, and was wearing slippers.

"Well, we're looking for a rock that glows in the dark," Jessie said.

"I don't believe that story. But I think we've lost Michael Running Deer now," Henry told her. "We can still check the dig, just in case." He turned up his collar against the cold night air. "Be as quiet as you can."

For the next few minutes, the children carefully picked their way through the forest. Violet felt as though she were walking on eggshells, and Benny shuffled behind her in his slippers.

"It's no use," Joe said when they arrived at the edge of the dig. "He's gone."

"Look over there!" Jessie's voice was strained. "There's a light under that tree!" She jabbed her finger at a spot several yards away.

Everyone turned to look, and Jessie said softly, "It's not a light exactly, is it? It looks more like . . . something glowing."

"A glowing rock!" Violet was excited. "Just like the one Ted Clark told us about!

He said it's a sign that there's buried treasure underneath."

"Let's go see — " Benny began, and then froze at an eerie sound whistling through the trees. "What's that?" he asked, clutching Violet's hand.

"I don't know," Violet said in a shaky voice.

"*Ooooooh . . . oooh.*" The low moan seemed to echo through the trees.

"Could it be an animal?" Jessie asked, drawing close to Amy.

"I don't think so," Amy answered. "I know the sounds of all the animals that live in this forest, and I've never heard anything like it." The sound seemed to circle them, sometimes loud, sometimes soft, just out of reach.

"We have to get out of here," Henry said firmly. "Right now."

"But what about the rock?" Joe protested.

"It will still be there tomorrow. Let's go." Amy was already making her way back through the forest, swinging her flashlight for the others. The noise stopped once they had reached the edge of the forest, and then the children broke into a dead run.

Once they reached the Lightfeather house, everyone headed for bed. "That was a close call," Violet said, tucking the Navajo blanket around her. "What do you think was making that noise?" she asked Amy.

Amy shook her head. "A person," she said, her voice serious. She was sitting up in bed, with her knees drawn up to her chest. "It was definitely a warning. Someone doesn't want us around the dig."

The next afternoon, Jessie went to the general store to mail a letter to Grandfather. She decided to stop by the stables on her way back to the Lightfeathers', and was surprised to see Rita Neville leading a sleek pinto horse out of the stable door.

"Be sure to keep a tight rein on Skywalker," Ed, the stable boy, was saying to her. "He loves to gallop, and if you're not careful, you'll find yourself flying."

"I'll remember that," Rita said, swinging herself up into the saddle. "I'll only be gone a couple of hours. I want to take a look at the mountains."

She spotted Jessie and gave a curt nod. Then she made a clucking noise, and the horse broke into a slow trot.

Jessie was heading for Thunder's stall, when she noticed a leather drawstring purse lying on the floor. Ed spotted it at the same time. "Darn! She forgot her purse."

"I'll take it to her," Jessie said quickly. She grabbed the purse and dashed out the door. Rita Neville was ambling down the trail behind the stables, and Jessie broke into a run, calling her name.

Ms. Neville reined in Skywalker, and headed back toward Jessie. "What is it?" she asked irritably, and then saw what Jessie was carrying. "Give me that!" She dug her heels into Skywalker's flanks, and he galloped to Jessie's side.

Why is she so angry? Jessie wondered. She started to lift the purse to Ms. Neville and then suddenly realized that the drawstring had come undone. A lipstick was lying on the ground, along with some loose change.

"Gosh, I'm sorry," Jessie said. When she bent down to retrieve the lipstick, Rita Neville dismounted in a cold fury.

"I said give it to me!" she repeated. She snatched the bag out of Jessie's hand and swung herself back into the saddle.

"Here's the lipstick and the coins," Jessie said.

Ms. Neville put out her hand, dropped the items into her purse, and angrily swung the reins. Skywalker obediently turned and headed away from Jessie, toward the mountains.

"She didn't even say thanks," Jessie muttered to herself. She started to walk toward the stable when she noticed a small glass bottle lying on the ground. Jessie picked it up and saw that it was nail polish. It had obviously fallen out of Ms. Neville's purse. After taking a quick look at Thunder, who was happily munching hay in his stall, Jessie decided to walk by the motel. She could return the nail polish and still be back at the Lightfeathers' by dinnertime.

At Morton's Motel, Jessie was disappointed that no one was on duty in the office. She was trying to decide what to do next, when a maid appeared with a pile of fresh towels.

"Just leave it outside her door," the maid suggested, when Jessie explained the problem. "She's staying in number twelve, the third door on the right."

"Thanks." When Jessie found room number twelve, she bent down to leave the nail polish on the door mat. Suddenly she realized that Ms. Neville's door was ajar. Inside, she could see Ted Clark looking in the closet. She drew back, shocked. He must have broken in! What was he looking for? Jessie quickly ducked out of sight and crept away.

After dinner that night, Jessie joined the rest of the children at the dining-room table and told them about her adventure. Benny was putting the finishing touches on his beadwork, and Henry was polishing silver belt buckles.

"I was so startled, I forgot to leave the nail polish," Jessie said at the end of the story. She reached into her pocket, and pulled out the small glass bottle. "That's funny," she said, turning it over in her hand. "I just realized it's empty."

"Why would someone carry around an empty bottle of nail polish?" Amy asked.

"It doesn't make sense," Violet said.

"Something else is funny," Jessie said. "Remember that key ring we found in the forest? Maybe the 'M' was for Morton's Motel!"

Henry looked up from his polishing. "So Rita Neville is definitely a suspect. She might be the one who's causing us so much trouble at the dig."

"But why?" Violet asked. "Why would a television producer want to interfere with what we're doing?"

"Maybe she's *not* a television producer," Jessie offered. "We only have her word for it. And she really acted strangely today."

"You know, we have quite a list of suspects," Amy said. "Ted Clark pretends he's part Navajo, but he knows nothing about our culture. He didn't even recognize turquoise."

"And he's not much of a genealogist. He didn't even know that Navajo tribes live in the Southwest," Joe added. "And what about Michael Running Deer? He's always snooping around the forest."

"But he has an excuse. He's working for the developer," Henry said.

"But there's no reason for him to be there in the middle of the night," Jessie pointed out. "I think Michael isn't what he seems."

"Do you think we should tell your parents about any of this?" Henry asked Joe.

"Not yet." Joe shook his head. "Mom and Dad are really involved with the Pow-Wow, and I'd hate to worry them."

"You're right," Amy agreed. "I think the best thing for us to do is keep our eyes open and work as hard as we can at the dig."

It was nearly eight o'clock that evening when Kinowok visited the Lightfeathers. "I've brought something special," he said, and handed Jessie a silver-and-turquoise necklace. "This belonged to my mother, and I would like you to wear it at the Pow-Wow."

"It's beautiful." Jessie ran her fingers over the bright bluish-green stones.

"It's a squash-blossom necklace," Amy told her. "And look at all the symbols carved in it."

"Do you know what each one means?" Kinowok asked.

Amy studied the necklace. "The coyote is respected for his wisdom, and the pipe stands for peace . . ."

"Look at that bird," Violet said. "It's just like the one on my bowl, and it even has a snake next to it."

"You found a dish with a thunderbird and a serpent?" Kinowok asked, his dark eyes alert.

"At the dig," Violet said. "It's the best thing we found."

"May I see it?" the old man asked.

"It was stolen." Violet's voice quivered a little.

Kinowok was silent. "This is very serious," he said softly.

"There's been a lot of really scary stuff going on!" Benny blurted out. "Someone's been sneaking around the forest at night, and we've heard funny noises."

"Do you think it is a man or a woman who is bothering you?" Kinowok sat down slowly and rested his chin on his hand.

"We followed a man through the forest one night," Henry told him.

"But one day we saw a woman's heel prints in the dirt," Amy offered. Everyone was silent for a moment, and Kinowok looked thoughtful.

"I think they want us to stop working on the dig," Joe said. "Sometimes they fill in the holes we've made, and other times they make them deeper. Maybe they're trying to find something, too."

"What do you think it means, Kinowok?" Amy asked.

"I think that you and your friends may have found something priceless," Kinowok told her.

"Like buried treasure?" Benny's eyes lit up.

"Better than treasure," Kinowok said. "You may have found the lost village."

CHAPTER 7

A Surprise Visit

"This doesn't look good," Mr. Lightfeather said the following morning. The whole family was gathered at the breakfast table, as he read a letter from the tribal council. "The developer has gotten his permit approved. He's going to start digging up the forest next week."

"Oh, no." Mrs. Lightfeather sat down slowly. She looked very upset. "I was afraid this would happen."

"Cheer up, Mom." Amy reached across the table to pat her mother's arm. "There's

still time for us to save the forest." She looked
at the Aldens encouragingly.

"We need to find something important at
the dig," Henry said thoughtfully. "Something that will prove that it's an historic site.
Then the real archaeologists can take over."

"I wish I still had my bowl," Violet said
glumly. "At least that was a start."

"What about the arrowheads I found?"
Benny asked.

"I'm afraid they're not enough, Benny,"
Mr. Lightfeather told him. "They prove that
people hunted there once, but we need to
show that they *lived* there."

The Aldens finished their breakfast
quickly, eager to get to the dig. "Maybe we'll
be lucky today," Violet said to Amy as they
cleared the table.

"I hope so," Amy answered. She glanced
out the kitchen window at the forest. It was
hard to believe that in a short time it might
be gone forever!

A half hour later, the Aldens were working
at the dig with Amy and Joe when Rita Neville appeared.

She stomped angrily over to Henry, and thrust a paper in his face. "I got your note," she said coldly.

"A note? What are you talking about?"

Rita gave a harsh laugh. "The one you kids slid under my door at the motel. If you think you're going to scare me off, you're wrong!"

"Ms. Neville, what are you talking about?" Amy asked.

"Read it for yourself!" Ms. Neville retorted. "Maybe you didn't write it, but one of your little friends did!"

Amy glanced at the paper Henry was holding. "*Stay away from the forest. There is danger in the shadows*," she read aloud. "Ms. Neville, we didn't write this!"

"Do you expect me to believe that?" Rita Neville stared at the group that was assembled around her. "I'll give you a little warning. The next time you bother me, you'll be the ones who are in danger!" She snatched the paper away from Henry, tore it into shreds, and threw it on the ground. Then, without another word, she turned and left.

"Wow," Benny said when she was out of sight. "She was really mad!"

"I wonder who wrote that note?" Jessie asked.

"I can't imagine," Joe said. "If none of us did it, who did?"

"Well, we're not going to figure it out by standing here," Henry reminded them. "Let's get back to work."

"Do you think we should look for that glowing rock we saw the other night?" Benny asked. "It was really creepy!"

"We can't take the time," Henry told him. "It's more important to look for artifacts."

Jessie picked up her shovel. "It probably only glows at night, Benny. We wouldn't have much chance of spotting it in the daylight."

It was mid-afternoon when Violet found a flat stone that was hollowed out on one side. "Is this anything important?" she asked Joe was was working a few feet away.

"It looks like a baking stone," he said, pleased.

"The Navajos used to bake stones?" Benny was puzzled.

Amy laughed. "No, they used stones to bake bread." She held the stone up so Benny could see it. "They used to build a fire here, under the rounded part. Then when the stone got hot underneath, the bread would cook on top."

"Maybe you should keep digging in the same area, Violet," Henry said. "In fact, I'll help you. It seems like you have the best square."

Henry and Violet worked side by side. They dug for a while. Henry uncovered part of a tomahawk. The handle was broken off, but the blade portion was in good condition.

"I can't believe it!" Amy said excitedly. "That's two finds in one day. Maybe we should all join Violet!"

"That's not a bad idea," Joe agreed. "She seems to be digging in the right spot, and she's dug down the deepest." Everyone started digging in the square next to Violet's and, half an hour later, Benny let out a whoop.

"Look what I found!" he said, holding up a handful of dazzling stones. They gleamed like jewels in the bright sunlight.

"What are they?" Violet asked.

"They're called butterfly stones," Amy explained. "We use them for jewelry." She turned one over. "You see how smooth the surface is? Someone polished them to bring out their true colors."

"Put them in the box, so they don't get chipped," Henry suggested.

The rest of the afternoon passed quickly, and Jessie found a stick that was beautifully carved and decorated with beads. "Oh, this is pretty," she said, brushing away clumps of dirt. "What is it?"

"It looks like a magic wand," Benny offered.

"That's close, Benny," Joe told him. "It's called a baton. It's a special wand that only the chiefs and the elders carry."

Jessie examined the beads that hung from threads. "These are beautiful," she said, admiring the little balls of quartz and copper. Suddenly she noticed some pointed white beads at the end of the string. "Wait a minute. These don't look like beads, they look like . . . teeth!"

Amy nodded. "I think they're probably from a wolf," she explained. "Our ancestors often used teeth for decoration." She smiled when Jessie made a face. "They thought that teeth were just as beautiful as beads."

"I think I have something!" Joe shouted. He threw down his trowel and began digging with his bare hands.

"What is it?" Amy said excitedly.

"It's some kind of a basket . . ." He lifted out a coiled basket that was lopsided. "It's heavy," he said, setting it down next to him.

"How come it's all black inside?" Benny asked, rushing over to take a look at it.

"That's pitch," Joe explained. "This is a cooking basket, right, Amy?"

Amy knelt down to examine it. "Yes, it is." She ran her hand around the smooth black interior. "This is the nicest one I've seen."

"How can you cook anything in a basket?" Violet asked.

"It's not an ordinary basket," Amy said. "The pitch makes the basket watertight. All you have to do is fill the basket with water and drop a heated stone in it. Once the water gets hot, you add the food."

After everyone had a look at the basket, Joe stood up and stretched. The sun was setting and a cool breeze had sprung up. "I think we should call it a day," he said. "It's almost dinnertime, and everybody's tired."

"And hungry!" Benny added, rubbing his legs. He felt cramped from squatting in one position so long.

Later that evening, Mr. and Mrs. Light-feather gathered in the dining room to admire the treasures.

"Do you think we have enough to convince people that there really is an ancient village?" Joe asked his mother.

"I think we have a good chance." She smiled and gave him a hug. "I still can't believe how much you children found today."

"What's going to happen next?" Violet asked.

"I think it's time to talk to the council," Mr. Lightfeather said. "In fact, we should call an emergency meeting."

"I'll speak to Kinowok soon," Mrs. Lightfeather offered. "Probably the best time to do it will be after the Pow-Wow."

"The Pow-Wow!" Benny said excitedly. "I almost forgot!"

"It's tomorrow," Joe reminded him. "Are you finished with your belt?"

"Almost," Benny said. "I just have three more rows of beads to do."

"We need to practice for the dance," Amy reminded Jessie. She glanced at her watch. "Do you want to work on it right now?"

"Yes, let's get started." Amy had promised her that the steps were simple, but Jessie still felt a little nervous about dancing in front of a lot of people.

"You'll see a lot of complicated dances at the Pow-Wow," Amy said a few minutes later. "But I've chosen an easy one for us to do." They were in Amy's bedroom, and a drumbeat was playing on a cassette deck.

"What do I do?" Jessie asked. She was

standing self-consciously in the center of the room.

"Just close your eyes for a minute and listen to the rhythm," Amy told her.

Jessie shut her eyes and listened. The drum beat was interesting and unusual. THUMP . . . thump, thump, thump. There seemed to be four beats and the first one was the loudest. She was surprised to find herself swaying to the music.

"Good," Amy said approvingly. "Now I'll show you how to do the Swan Dance." She opened her dresser drawer and pulled out two bright orange shawls. She handed one to Jessie. "Step side to side, and raise and lower the shawl. Do it really slowly so the shawl drifts in the air for a moment."

Amy and Jessie stood side by side, moving to the music. Jessie was so interested she forgot to be nervous. "Bow your head a little when the shawl comes down," Amy added. Jessie followed her movements and, when the song ended, Amy applauded. "You dance just like a Navajo girl," she said happily.

It was almost nine o'clock when Mr. Lightfeather summoned Joe and Henry. "How about a hand with these boxes?" he asked. "I've packed all the artifacts you found at the dig. I think we should put everything in the basement for safekeeping."

"I'll help!" Benny offered.

"I think you need to finish your belt," Joe said gently. "You still have one more row of beads to do."

"I guess you're right." Benny wanted to take a last look at the tomahawk, but he knew it was more important to finish his belt.

Joe and Henry carried six sturdy cardboard boxes downstairs, and Mr. Lightfeather unlocked a green metal storage container. After they arranged the boxes on the shelves, Mr. Lightfeather closed the sliding door and snapped the padlock shut. The noise echoed in the dimly lit cellar. "At least we know they'll be safe in here," Joe said.

"That's right, son," his father agreed. "And as soon as the Pow-Wow is over, we'll present them to the tribal council. Once they see the artifacts, the council will stop the developers in their tracks!"

CHAPTER 8

Benny's Discovery

It was nearly midnight when Benny came to a decision — he just *had* to take one last look at the treasures from the dig. After making sure that Joe and Henry were sound asleep, he crept out of the bedroom and headed downstairs. He groped his way in the dark to the kitchen, and was just about to open the basement door when he heard a loud *CLUNK*. Someone was in the basement! His heart racing, he cracked open the door and peeked downstairs. A shadowy figure was standing in front of a storage cab-

inet, fumbling with a padlock. Benny craned his neck for a better view and suddenly realized who it was — Rita Neville!

Had she spotted him? Benny closed the door and leaned against it for a moment, too scared to breathe. Then he tiptoed out of the kitchen, being careful not to bump into anything. He hurried upstairs and burst into his bedroom.

"Henry! Wake up!" He shook his brother's arm and Henry sat up slowly.

"What's wrong?" Joe called from the next bunk. His voice was groggy with sleep.

"Rita Neville! She broke into the house. She's downstairs in the basement . . . stealing our stuff from the dig!"

Instantly awake, Henry bounded out of bed, as Joe flipped on the light. "I'll wake up my parents," Joe said quietly.

"And I'll go tell the girls," Henry added. "Benny, you'd better come with me."

Henry and Benny padded quietly down the hall into the girls' room. He had just finished telling them what was happening when Mrs. Lightfeather appeared with Joe. She closed the door and locked it, then turned to face the children. "We have to be very quiet," she said. Her voice was low and urgent. "My husband's calling the police right now. He wants us to stay in here until they arrive."

"How many burglars are there?" Violet asked. She shivered a little and pulled her bathrobe tightly around her.

"Ms. Neville's the only one I saw," Benny said. "But there might be more." He edged closer to Jessie. "They could be sneaking around the rest of the house right now. They could be coming to get us!"

Jessie pulled him close to her. "I think it's the artifacts they want. Not us."

They huddled silently together for the next few minutes, and then suddenly Benny heard a car drive up behind the house. He pulled away and dashed to the bedroom window. "It's the police!"

"They didn't use the siren or the lights," Jessie said, joining him. "I bet they don't want to scare anybody off."

Everyone watched as three uniformed officers got out of the car and approached the house. They saw Mr. Lightfeather talking to them in the backyard, and then two of the officers trooped inside with him. The third one was shining his flashlight into the bushes around the garden.

"I wonder what — " Violet began.

"Put your hands up, and keep them up!" someone shouted from downstairs.

"Wow — they're arresting somebody!" Benny said. He was just about to ask if he could go take a peek, when Mr. Lightfeather called through the door into the bedroom. "Everyone okay in here?"

"We're fine," Mrs. Lightfeather assured him, opening the door. "But what's happening down there?"

"It was Rita Neville," Mr. Lightfeather said. His hair was rumpled and he was wearing jeans and a pajama top. "And they got her." He put his arm around Benny's shoulders. "It's a good thing you decided to go down to the basement when you did, son. She was all set to walk off with everything."

"What happens now?" Henry asked.

"We have to give a statement to the police," Mr. Lightfeather said.

Everyone followed Mr. Lightfeather downstairs, where one of the officers was speaking into a walkie-talkie. Ms. Neville was already in the squad car.

"Why don't we sit at the dining-room table?" Mr. Lightfeather suggested.

The officer joined them at the table and flipped open a notebook. Suddenly, his walkie-talkie squawked. "Excuse me," he said, lifting it to his ear. He listened intently for a few minutes, with a grim look on his face. "Another one! Well, bring him in," he ordered.

"What's wrong?" Mr. Lightfeather asked.

"It looks like there was someone else involved. Officer Davis found a man hiding in your backyard."

"So Rita Neville had a partner, after all," Henry said thoughtfully.

"But who?" Violet asked.

"Ted Clark," a voice said loudly behind her. "At least that's what he says his name is." Everyone turned around to see Ted Clark, in handcuffs, standing next to a young police officer.

Benny could hardly believe it. Two criminals had been caught just because he had started down to the basement!

"He told us he was researching his roots," Amy said. "He said he was part Navajo, but I never really believed him."

Suddenly Violet noticed something suspicious. There was red clay all over Ted's shoes and trousers — the same kind of clay they had found in the forest!

Joe noticed it at the same time. "You must have been sneaking around the dig," he said accusingly.

"The dig?" The officer looked puzzled.

"Our archaeological dig," Henry explained. "That's where we found all the artifacts."

"Well, that explains why he was carrying a shovel when we spotted him," the policeman said. "When he and Rita Neville didn't find anything left at your dig, they must have decided to check out the house."

"I don't understand," Henry said slowly. "What do you have to do with Rita Neville?"

"We're married," Ted Clark said. "We've been looking all over for artifacts. We'd heard about the lost village."

"They're wanted for grand theft," the policeman said. "They work together."

"So that's why you were hanging around the dig and asking questions," Jessie said. "You hoped we'd find something valuable."

"And Rita Neville isn't really a television producer, is she?" Amy said.

"Take him into town and book him," the officer at the table said to his young partner. "And Rita, too. She's in the squad car."

"Wait," Jessie said suddenly. "There's something I have to know." She walked over to Ted Clark. "One night we saw a glowing rock in the woods, just like the legend said. We never saw it again. Did you and Rita have something to do with that?"

"Oh, yeah, the glowing rock," Ted said. "She figured you'd fall for that. We wanted to throw you off the track, so we could work at the dig in peace."

"There really was a glowing rock?" Benny asked.

"Sure there was," Ted said. "Thanks to a little iridescent nail polish."

"The nail polish!" Suddenly Jessie remembered how upset Rita Neville had been when Jessie had found her purse. And that explained why the bottle was empty. Rita had used it all up, painting the rock!

"You and Rita were in the woods that night," Amy said. "You tried to scare us off."

"Sure we were," Ted told her. "We were trying to uncover some things at the dig. I thought the glowing rock would lead you off in the wrong direction, but when you started to get too close to the dig, we began howling."

"Those were the sounds we heard!" Benny said.

It was another hour before the police finished interviewing the Lightfeathers and the Aldens. Benny was yawning, but he felt tired and excited all at the same time. So much had happened!

And the next day was the Pow-Wow!

CHAPTER 9

The Pow-Wow

"I hope you made plenty of fried bread," Joe said to his mother a few hours later. The family had gathered in the kitchen for a quick breakfast before the Pow-Wow.

"We made five baskets to bring with us," Violet said, "and we saved some just for you." She pointed to the heavy cast-iron skillet where squares of bread dough were sizzling to a rich golden brown.

"May I try some?" Benny asked. With tongs, Violet carefully lifted a square of bread out of the pan. Then she dipped it in powdered sugar and handed it to him on a napkin.

"Maybe you'd better take it with you, son," Mr. Lightfeather said, glancing at his watch. "It's getting late, and we don't want to miss the opening ceremony."

They quickly loaded the van, and Benny made a dash upstairs for his belt. He wanted to display it at the Pow-Wow, but he knew he'd never sell it. It meant too much to him.

When everyone was finally settled in the van, Benny realized that Jessie and Amy were wearing their buckskin dresses. "Wow, you've got real Navajo costumes," he said admiringly.

"We call it regalia," Amy corrected him gently. "Jessie and I will be dancing right after the Grand Entry."

The area chosen for the Pow-Wow was in a clearing at the edge of the forest. Joe had explained to the Aldens that one special area was roped off in a circle. It was holy ground and had been blessed by the elders of the tribe. All the dancing and ceremonial rites would be held there.

Mr. Lightfeather parked the van in a field, and the children jumped out excitedly. "Look how many cars there are," Amy said to Joe. "It looks like the whole town has turned out for the Pow-Wow."

The Aldens helped the Lightfeathers set up a folding table and arrange the trays of traditional Navajo dishes — corn bread, chili fritters, and stuffed sweet peppers.

"We'd better hurry," Mrs. Lightfeather said. "It's almost time for the Grand Entry." After making a final check of the table, everyone headed for the roped-off area, passing dozens of booths filled with Navajo jewelry and pottery.

"Look, there's Kinowok," Henry pointed out. He spotted the elderly leader in full regalia, leading a group of men and women toward the circle.

"He'll say the opening blessing," Joe explained. "Then we'll have the inter-tribal dances."

Jessie felt a little nervous when she heard the drumbeat, but Amy squeezed her hand reassuringly. "It's okay," she whispered.

"We're the last ones on the schedule."

"That gives me more time to worry," Jessie whispered back.

Amy laughed. "Just enjoy watching the dancers. And when it's our turn, forget the crowd and pretend you're back in my room."

The people bowed their heads for the blessing, and then four spirited young men performed the Snake Dance in the center of the ring. The drumbeat became faster as they advanced and retreated to the edge of the ropes.

"The Snake Dance is my favorite part of the Pow-Wow," Joe confided to Henry.

"Why would anyone want to dance like a snake?" Benny asked.

"The snake is very important to us because he lives close to the ground," Amy told him. "Whenever the soil is dry and parched, he can send a message to the gods." She smiled. "At least, that's what our ancestors thought."

The Aldens watched the dancing for over an hour, and then Jessie heard the Swan Dance being announced over a loudspeaker.

"That's us," Amy said, tugging at her arm.

"Don't forget your shawl," she added as she ducked under the rope and into the ring.

She and Jessie stood perfectly still, waiting until the drum began beating a familiar rhythm. Then, right on cue, both girls swayed back and forth, the fringe on their outfits floating on the crisp breeze. Jessie moved through the steps easily, and was so caught up in the music, she forgot to be nervous. When the song was over, she was startled by the burst of applause.

"You were great!" Amy whispered, as they rejoined the family.

"What's next?" Benny said. He liked watching the dances, especially the ones with spears and shields, but he was hungry.

"How about an early lunch?" Mrs. Lightfeather suggested.

"C'mon," Joe offered. "I'll take you on a tour of the food booths."

"Can we start over there? Whatever he's making sure smells good." Benny pointed to a man cooking over an open fire.

Joe looked over his shoulder and nodded. "That's Bobbie Redbird from the Ute tribe.

And you'll never guess what he's cooking — tortillas!"

"Let's go!" Benny yelled, scampering away.

"Mom, would you like to walk around with Dad for a while?" Amy offered. She glanced at her friends. "Jessie and Violet and I can take care of our booth."

"That would be nice," Mrs. Lightfeather said, linking her arm through her husband's. "We only get to see some of our friends once a year at the Pow-Wow."

After lunch, all the children visited a craft booth, and Henry picked up a strange-looking object. It was a round wooden hoop with gauzy threads woven back and forth through the center. "What's this?" he asked, puzzled.

"Oh, that's a dream catcher," Joe said. "We always kept one in our bedrooms when we were little."

"But what's it for?"

Joe grinned. "It lets the good dreams in and keeps the bad ones out."

"I think I'll buy one," Benny said. "Then

I'll never get nightmares again."

"Let's all buy one," Jessie suggested. She was looking over the selection when Kinowok and Michael Running Deer approached them. Jessie noticed that Michael was wearing a beaded necklace with his denim shirt.

"That was very fine dancing," Kinowok said to Jessie. His brown eyes were twinkling as he solemnly shook hands with her. "I think you should become an honorary member of our tribe."

"I told her she dances like a Navajo," Amy said proudly.

"And you, Benny, are you enjoying the Pow-Wow?" Kinowok rested his hand on the young boy's shoulder.

"I sure am!" Benny whirled around in a circle waving his dream catcher in the air. "Did you hear what happened last night?" he blurted out. "We had police cars and everything at the house. It was scary!"

"What happened?" Kinowok's voice was serious, and Michael Running Deer stepped closer.

Henry briefly told them what had happened, and finished with a description of Ted Clark and Rita Neville being arrested.

"It's just as I suspected," Kinowok said. He leaned on his walking stick, and looked sad. "In their greed, they thought of the artifacts as treasure. They didn't understand the real importance of them. They tried to steal a part of our history."

"Then you think we've really discovered the ancient village?" Joe asked.

Kinowok nodded. "I feel very certain of it. I suspected Rita Neville was not trustworthy so when I knew you were getting close, I urged her to leave the reservation. If she had heeded my warning, she and Ted Clark both would be free now."

"You warned her?" Amy asked.

"Of course — the note!" Violet said, suddenly understanding. "You must have written that note to Rita. She accused us of putting it under her door at the motel."

Kinowok tapped his chest with his palm. "I did it. I wanted to give them one last chance to leave us alone." He shrugged. "But they ignored my plea, and now they must pay the price."

"At least it's all over now," Henry said.

"That's right," Joe offered. "Tomorrow Mom and Dad are going to bring all the artifacts to the town council. Once the judge sees what we've found, he'll protect the forest. Then someone can start a real excavation and find the lost village."

"Unless the developer tries to fight it," Amy said.

"I don't think he will," Henry said. "Not if he realizes what's at stake."

Kinowok looked at Michael Running Deer. "Is that true, my friend? You work for the developer. Will he leave quietly once he learns about the ancient village?"

Michael looked directly into the old man's eyes. "I don't know what will happen," he said softly. "It's not up to me."

"I understand." Kinowok patted him on the shoulder. "Some things are out of your hands." He smiled at the children. "Tomorrow will be here soon enough. Let's enjoy the rest of the Pow-Wow."

The day passed quickly for the Aldens. Mrs. Lightfeather sold all of the baked goods she brought, and Joe sold half a dozen beaded belts. Both Benny and Henry had decided to keep the belts they had made.

It was late afternoon when the men performed the Spear and Shield Dance to close the Pow-Wow. Benny sat cross-legged on the ground and watched as two warriors in full regalia pretended to do battle in the center of the ring. At the end, one of them waved his spear and moved into a fast war dance as the drumbeats reached a climax.

Then everyone held hands as they joined in a closing song, watching as the huge bonfire turned to embers.

"I'll always remember this, won't you?" Violet whispered to Jessie.

Jessie nodded, swaying to the music. She knew that she would never forget her Navajo friends and everything they had taught her.

CHAPTER 10

A Day in Court

Benny woke up after everyone else the next morning, and the aroma of sizzling bacon lured him downstairs. Mrs. Lightfeather smiled when she saw his rumpled hair and motioned him to a seat at the breakfast table.

"Don't worry, Benny," she assured him. "We saved plenty of hotcakes for you."

"But eat fast," Joe said, draining his glass of orange juice. "Dad's already loading the artifacts into the truck. The council meeting starts in half an hour."

The phone rang, and Mrs. Lightfeather hurried to answer it. After a brief conversation, she looked very happy and took Violet's hand in hers. "I have a wonderful surprise for you, Violet. The police found your bowl. It's going to be part of the evidence this morning."

"They found my bowl?" Violet was thrilled. She knew she couldn't keep it, but she was glad it would help prove their case.

"Rita Neville had it stashed away in her motel room. It's in perfect condition, and one of the elders says it looks like it was made a long time ago. It's priceless."

"Are they going to look at my arrowheads?" Benny asked.

"Sure they are," Joe told him. "And they may even let you keep one, right, Mom?"

"Maybe," Mrs. Lightfeather answered. "That's for the elders to decide."

"Is this going to be like a real trial?" Violet asked. She felt a little nervous and wondered if she would have to tell her story in front of a room full of people.

"No, it's more like a hearing. All the elders

will be there, and they've invited a local judge to attend. He's the only one who can order the developer to stop."

"The site will be preserved," said Amy.

"If he agrees it's worth saving," Henry said.

"Everybody ready?" Mr. Lightfeather suddenly appeared in the doorway.

"We're on our way!" Benny grabbed a piece of bacon and scooted off his chair. He hoped he could show off his arrowheads.

The council meeting was held in the main lodge. Dozens of people were already seated in the large, airy hall when the Aldens trooped in with the Lightfeathers.

Mr. Lightfeather and the others carefully placed the artifacts on a long wooden table in the front of the room. As soon as they were finished, Kinowok rapped his gavel and called the meeting to order. Joe noticed that a gray-haired woman in a dark suit was standing next to Kinowok at the podium.

"Please be seated," he said, pointing to a row of folding chairs. "I'd like the Aldens and the Lightfeathers to sit up front, so they can testify, if need be."

Kinowok waited until everyone had sat down, and then introduced his guest. "This is Judge Tompkins, from Superior Court," he said. There was a low murmur of approval from the crowd when the gray-haired woman nodded. "I think most of you know her, and know that she is a fair woman. She is here today to hear our story, to see our evidence, and to decide the fate of our forest." Kinowok paused. I turn this meeting over to the judge." He handed the gavel to Judge Tompkins and took his seat with the tribal elders.

"What happens now?" Benny whispered to Amy.

"I guess we'll have a chance to tell her about the artifacts — " she began, when a noise at the back of the room distracted her.

"Look who's here!" Violet said in a low voice. She watched in surprise as Michael Running Deer walked swiftly up the center aisle and took a seat in the front row. "I wonder why he showed up?"

"Probably to hurt our case," Amy said glumly. "Don't forget, he works for the developer."

"I'd like to start by examining the evidence," Judge Tompkins said. She motioned to Mr. Lightfeather. "Please hold up the items one at a time." She smiled at the six children in the front row. "I understand that you found all of these items in the forest that borders the reservation?"

"We sure did!" Benny blurted out. "We dug up every single one of them. I found the arrowheads," he added proudly, and a ripple of laughter went through the room.

"Kinowok tells me that this is strong evidence that a village once existed on the site," the judge said. "It's very fortunate that you found these objects."

After all the artifacts had been described and examined, the tribal elders met privately with the judge in a small anteroom.

"What do you think they'll decide?" Henry asked Mr. Lightfeather.

"I think Judge Tompkins was impressed, but you never know how these things will go," Mr. Lightfeather told him. "After all, the developer will tell his side of the story. If he builds homes on the site, it will bring a lot of new jobs into the area."

"Sssh, they're coming back," said Mrs. Lightfeather.

"The elders are smiling," Joe said. "Do you think that's good news?"

"I hope so," his mother answered.

Judge Tompkins returned to the podium and looked over the crowd. "I've seen some very convincing evidence this morning, and there isn't much doubt that the forest is an important site. Is it worth preserving, worth protecting? According to my young friends" — she gestured to the six children — "the answer is yes. But I must be fair. I must consider all sides of the issue."

Judge Tompkins adjusted her glasses and looked over a document in front of her on the podium. "And so in the interest of fairness, I had to ask myself a very important question: Is it important for the Navajo people to know how their ancestors lived? How they hunted, and gathered food, and played with their children?" She paused, and then folded her hands. "The answer is yes. It is very important that this knowledge not be lost for all time. The ancient village — if it really exists — could answer many of these questions. The village must be saved!"

A gasp went up from the audience, and Benny was so excited he almost jumped out of his chair. Judge Tompkins rapped the gavel to restore order. "I am hereby declaring the forest an historic site. It is protected by law from development, and you may continue your excavations." She turned over the gavel to Kinowok. "Good luck," she said to the old man. "Let me know when you find the village and I will celebrate with you."

Kinowok took his place in front of the podium. "I thank all of you for coming today," he said, his voice strong. "And I thank our new friends, the Aldens, for their help. You have added much to our lives, and you have our friendship. The council meeting is over."

"Is that it?" Violet asked. The elders left the lodge first, and then everyone began filing down the center aisle.

"Not quite," Joe said. "Michael Running

Deer is heading straight for us!"

"I wonder what he wants?" Amy said.

The Lightfeathers and the Aldens had just reached the door when Michael Running Deer intercepted them. He stood in front of them, barring their way. "Wait a minute, please," he said. "I need to talk to you."

"If you want to ruin the forest, it's too late," Joe said. "We won. You'll have to build your vacation homes someplace else."

Michael looked embarrassed. "No, that's not what I want to say at all. I don't work for the developer anymore."

"You don't? What happened?" Mrs. Light-feather looked surprised.

He shrugged. "I'm a full-blooded Navajo, just like you, and I suddenly realized that I couldn't hurt my own people." He looked at the children. "When I saw all of you work-ing at the dig, it reminded me of a dream I had. I wanted to be an archaeologist once. I even studied archaeology in college, but then I got sidetracked." He held open the front door, and they all stepped out into the bright sunlight. "Now I see that I can still go after my dream. I'm going to help with the dig."

"Michael's decision was certainly a surprise," Mrs. Lightfeather said later when they were in their truck, heading home.

"A nice one!" Amy said with a laugh.

"What happens now?" Henry asked.

Mrs. Lightfeather glanced at her watch. "We just have time to have a quick lunch at home before your grandfather comes to pick you up."

Grandfather! Violet thought. She was looking forward so much to seeing him, but she knew she would miss the Lightfeathers. Amy and Joe promised to write and tell her what was happening at the dig, but it wouldn't be the same as being there.

It was early afternoon when a taxi pulled into the Lightfeathers' driveway and Grandfather got out.

"Grandfather's here!" Violet cried, running to meet him.

"It's been a long two weeks without you,

children," he said, hugging each of the Aldens in turn.

"We missed you, too, Grandfather," Jessie said. "But so much has happened!"

"You'll have to tell me all about it on the plane," Grandfather said. "We just have time to get to the airport."

Violet and Amy looked at each other. "How can we say good-bye?" Violet said, giving her a hug.

"We'll keep in touch. We'll write lots of letters," Amy promised.

"Thanks for taking care of the children," Grandfather said to the Lightfeathers. "I know it was a wonderful experience for them."

"It was quite an experience for us!" Mrs. Lightfeather said, smiling. "In fact, I'd say it was absolutely amazing."

"Really?" Grandfather looked puzzled. "Did something interesting happen here?"

The Aldens and the Lightfeathers laughed. "Interesting? Just wait until you hear the whole story!" Benny said.

GERTRUDE CHANDLER WARNER discovered when she was teaching that many readers who like an exciting story could find no books that were both easy and fun to read. She decided to try to meet this need, and her first book, *The Boxcar Children*, quickly proved she had succeeded.

Miss Warner drew on her own experiences to write the mystery. As a child she spent hours watching trains go by on the tracks opposite her family home. She often dreamed about what it would be like to set up housekeeping in a caboose or freight car — the situation the Alden children find themselves in.

When Miss Warner received requests for more adventures involving Henry, Jessie, Violet, and Benny Alden, she began additional stories. In each, she chose a special setting and introduced unusual or eccentric characters who liked the unpredictable.

While the mystery element is central to each of Miss Warner's books, she never thought of them as strictly juvenile mysteries. She liked to stress the Aldens' independence and resourcefulness and their solid New England devotion to using up and making do. The Aldens go about most of their adventures with as little adult supervision as possible — something else that delights young readers.

Miss Warner lived in Putnam, Connecticut, until her death in 1979. During her lifetime, she received hundreds of letters from girls and boys telling her how much they liked her books.